Dar

Second series

The Dark Candle	978-184167-603-6
The Dark Machine	978-184167-601-2
The Dark Words	978-184167-602-9
Dying for the Dark	978-184167-604-3
Killer in the Dark	978-184167-605-0
The Day is Dark	978-184167-606-7
The Dark River	978-184167-745-3
The Bridge of Dark Tears	978-184167-746-0
The Past is Dark	978-184167-747-7
Playing the Dark Game	978-184167-748-4
The Dark Music	978-184167-749-1
The Dark Garden	978-184167-750-7

First series

The Dark Fire of Doom	978-184167-417-9
Destiny in the Dark	978-184167-422-3
The Dark Never Hides	978-184167-419-3
The Face in the Dark Mirror	978-184167-411-7
Fear in the Dark	978-184167-412-4
Escape from the Dark	978-184167-416-2
Danger in the Dark	978-184167-415-5
The Dark Dreams of Hell	978-184167-418-6
The Dark Side of Magic	978-184167-414-8
The Dark Glass	978-184167-421-6
The Dark Waters of Time	978-184167-413-1
The Shadow in the Dark	978-184167-420-9

Dark Man

The Dark Music
by Peter Lancett
illustrated by Jan Pedroietta

Published by Ransom Publishing Ltd.
Radley House, 8 St. Cross Road, Winchester, Hampshire, UK
SO23 9HX
www.ransom.co.uk

ISBN   978 184167 749 1

First published in 2011

Copyright © 2011 Ransom Publishing Ltd.

Text copyright © 2011 Peter Lancett
Illustrations copyright © 2011 Jan Pedroietta

Dark Man

The Dark Music

by Peter Lancett

illustrated by Jan Pedroietta

Ransom

Chapter One:
The Piano

In the bad part of the city, the buildings look ruined.

Even so, people live in these buildings.

Mostly they are good people, but there is a lot of crime here.

Angela lives here, a killer with an evil heart.

She lives in a run-down flat in a run-down building.

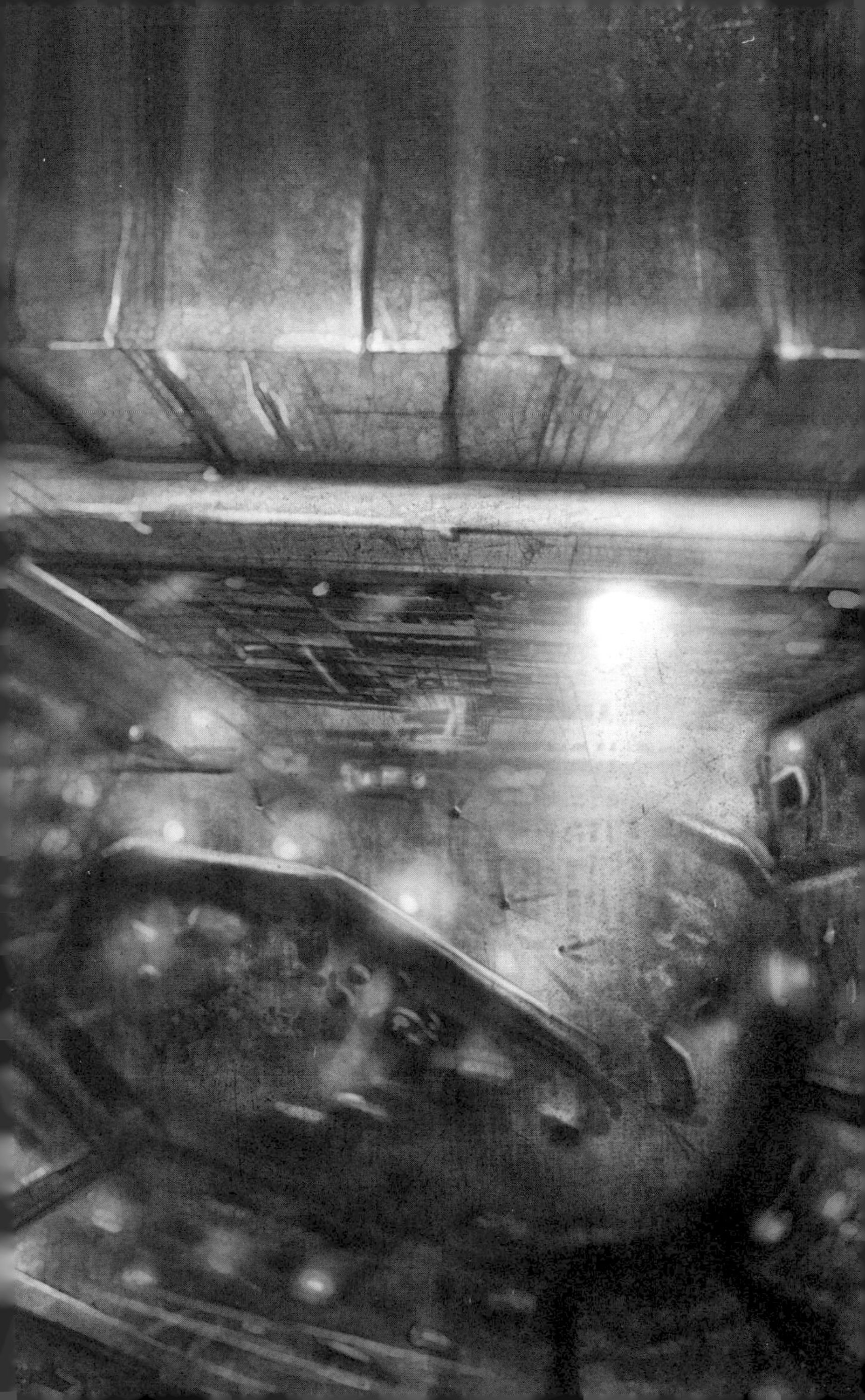

It is night and the Dark Man has come to visit Angela.

In Angela's flat, the Dark Man stands by the window.

Angela stands well back. She is nervous.

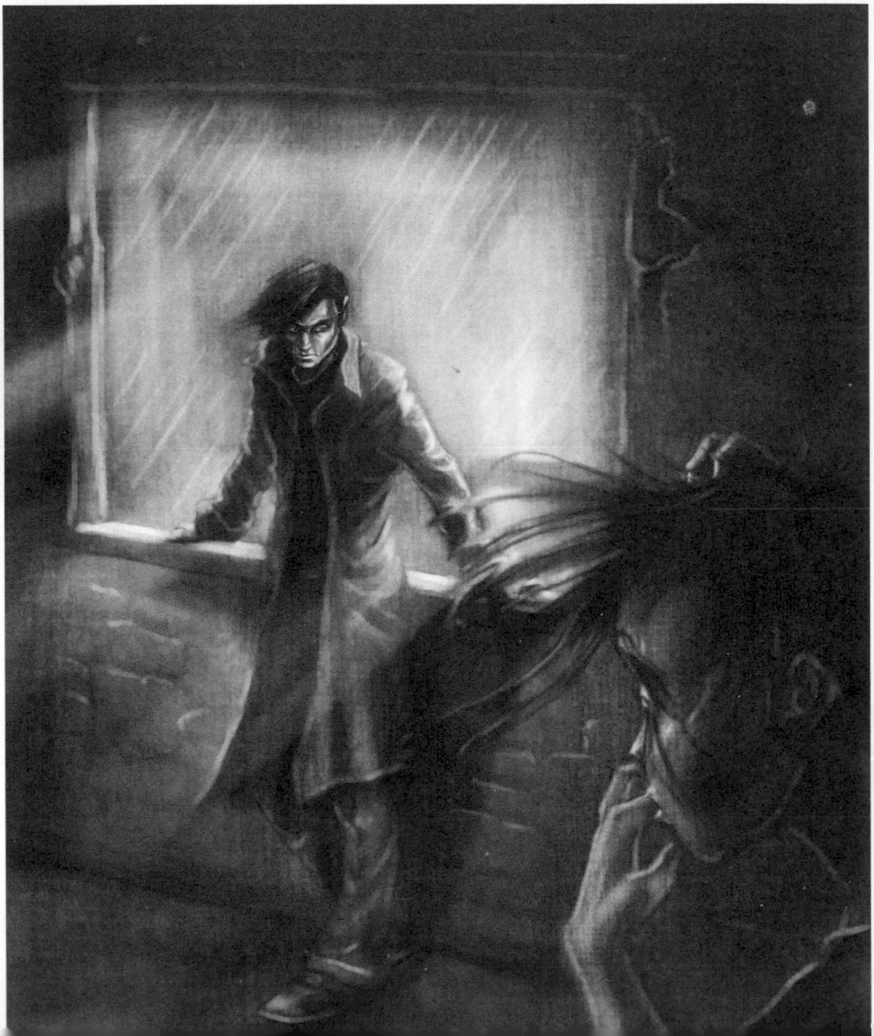

The Dark Man looks down to the street, several floors below.

'There, can you hear it?' Angela asks.

The Dark Man listens.

Through the cracked glass, he can just hear the notes of a piano.

The music is fast and never stops.

It is not pretty music.

'It is coming from there,' Angela says, pointing at a tall, rotten building two blocks away.

The Dark Man looks over at the building.

There is a dirty, yellow light in one window on the top floor.

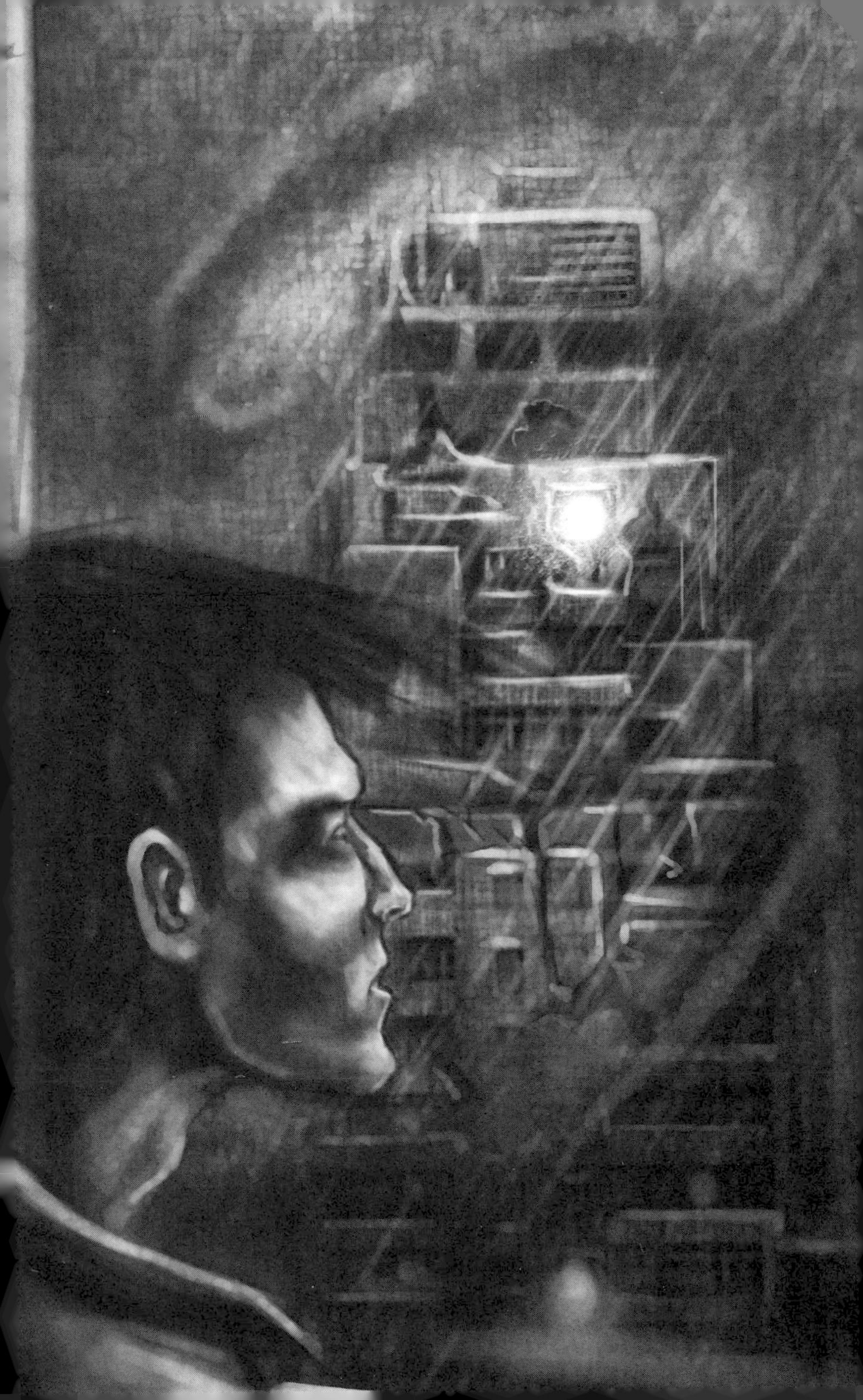

The Dark Man turns to Angela.

'Who lives there?' he asks.

Angela is afraid.

'Nobody,' she says. 'The building is not real!'

The Dark Man sees that Angela is holding a kitchen knife.

'Do something,' Angela says. 'It is driving me mad!'

The Dark Man nods slowly.

'I will take a look,' he says. 'Do not leave this room until I return.'

Chapter Two:
The Children

Out on the streets, the Dark Man heads towards the building.

He can just hear the notes of the awful music above the wind.

The music seems to call to him.

The streets are mostly empty, but he sees children; not many, but in twos and threes.

Some are holding hands.

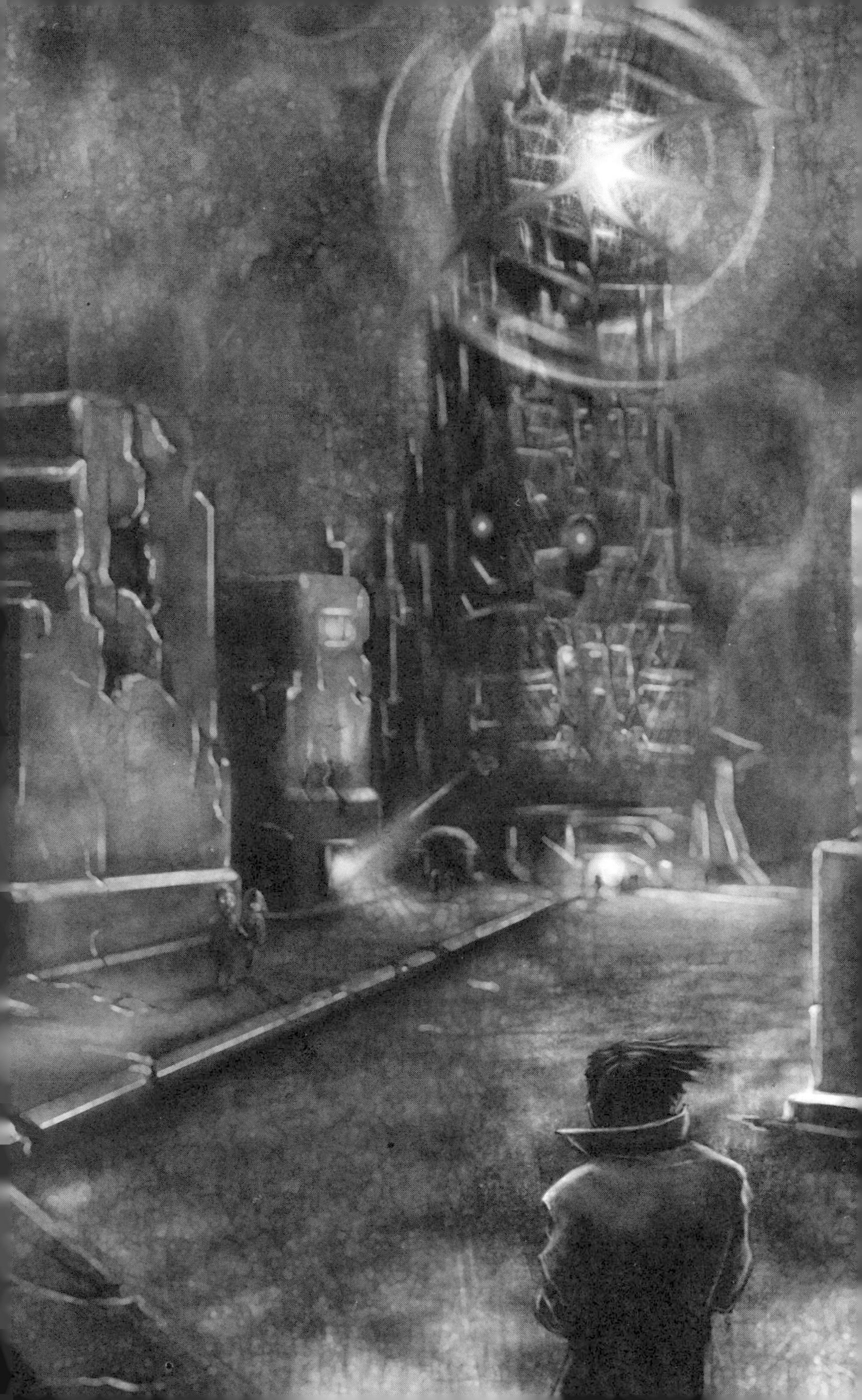

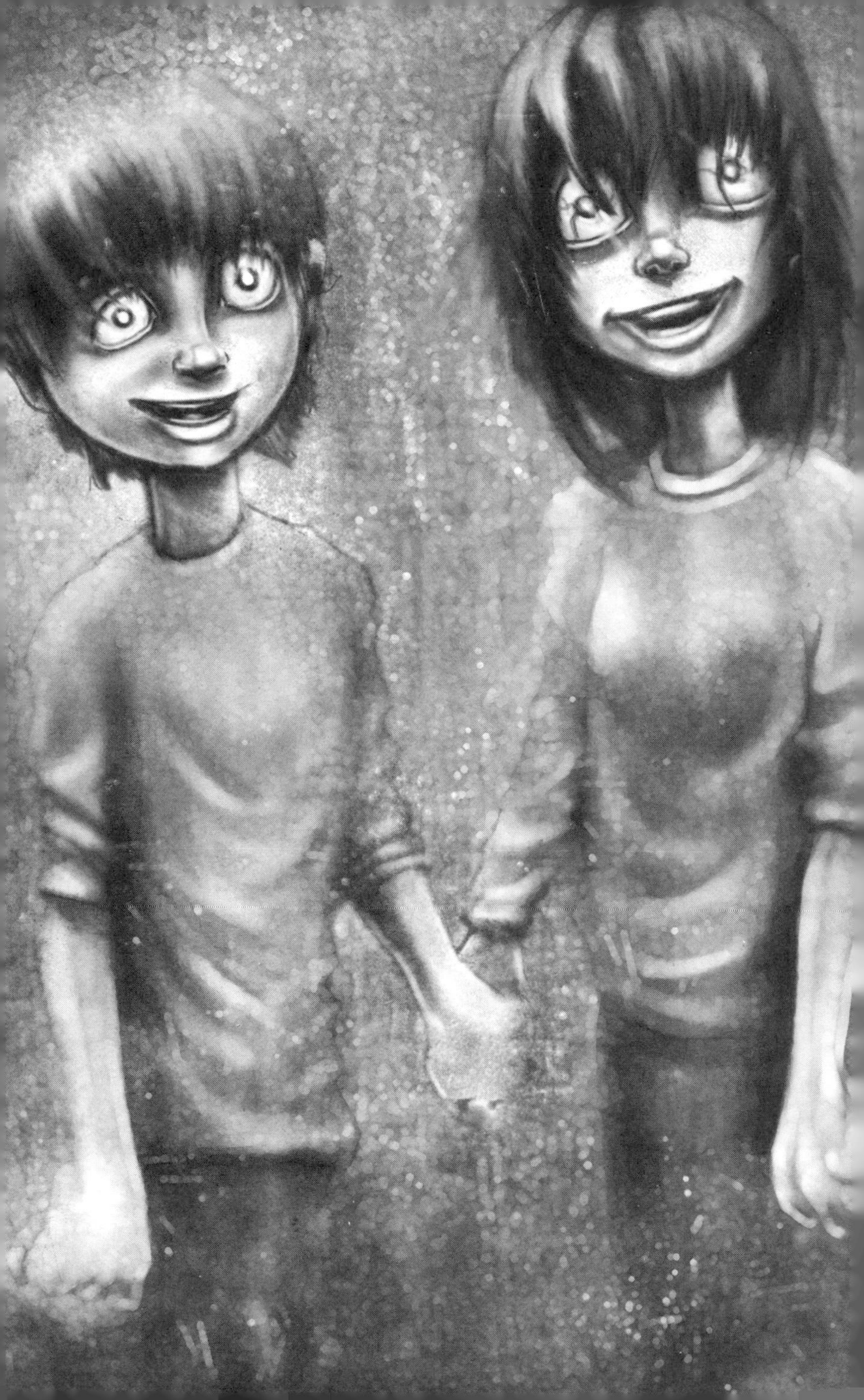

The children are smiling and seem drawn towards the music.

The Dark Man knows that something bad is happening.

He lets the music pull him, and follows the children.

The music does not get louder, but its pull gets stronger.

And the nearer he gets, the darker the night becomes.

As he turns a corner, the horrible building is suddenly before him.

The pull of the music is so strong that he has to hold on to a door frame.

The children are running towards the dark building.

Other children are coming out. These children do not look happy.

They shuffle slowly and their eyes just stare.

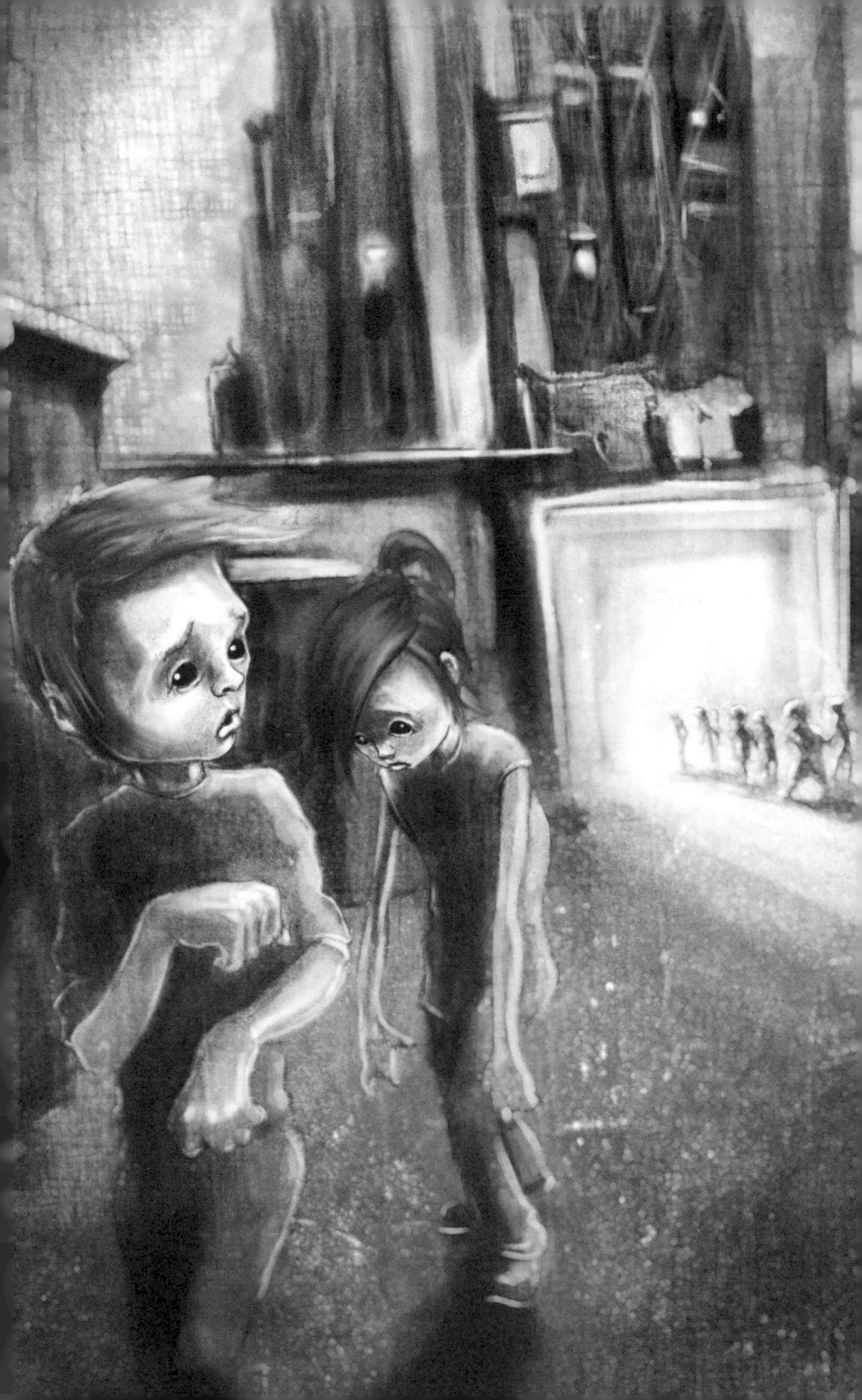

The music has stolen their happiness.

The Dark Man claps his hands over his ears to block the music out.

The music no longer pulls him, but he will have to come back tomorrow, when it is light.

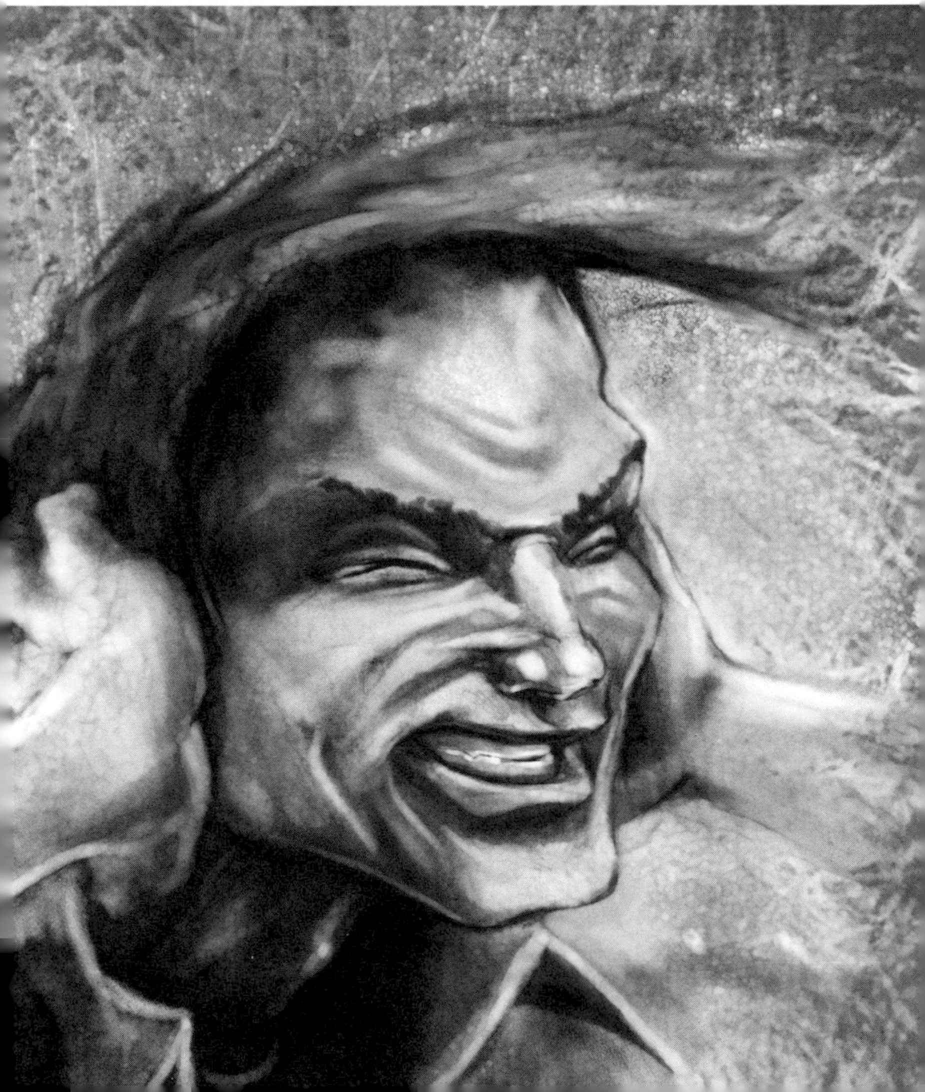

The music is taking strength from the darkness.

No wonder it is driving Angela mad.

Chapter Three:
Only the Music Lives Here

Next morning, the Dark Man returns to the terrible building.

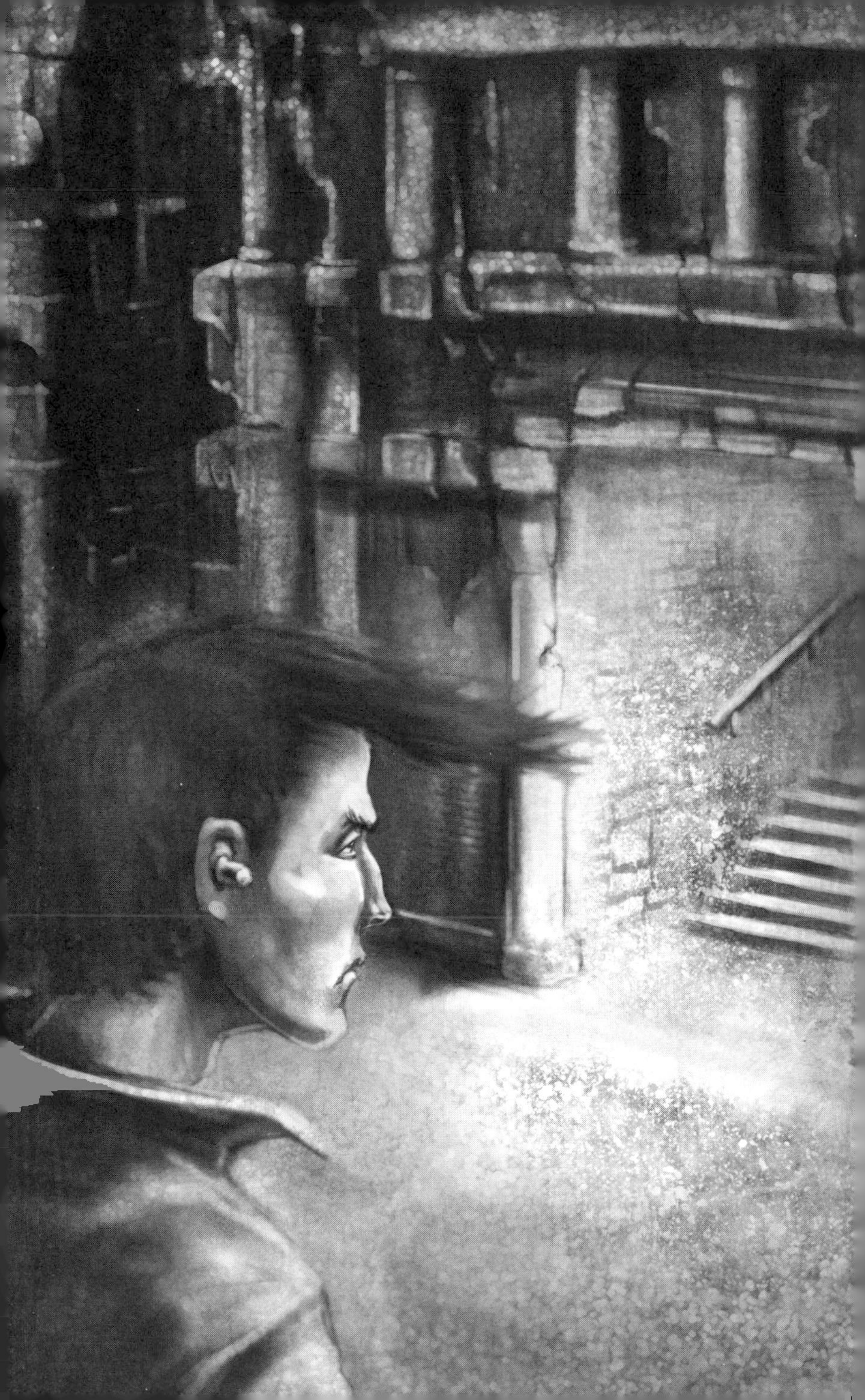

He checks several times that this is the right street, but the building seems much smaller now.

Last night it had been higher, climbing way up into the night sky.

The Dark Man is wearing ear plugs.

He cannot hear the sounds of the city as he enters the building.

The hallway is gloomy and derelict.

At the far end there is an elevator, but it looks broken.

The Dark Man begins to climb the stairs.

As he climbs, it gets darker, even though he can see daylight outside the windows.

None of that light seems to come into the building.

On the third floor landing, the Dark Man sees a little boy, sitting with his back to the wall.

The little boy seems sad and his eyes just stare.

'Do you live here?' the Dark Man asks.

The little boy does not look up, but he says something.

The Dark Man cannot hear, so he takes the ear plugs from his ears.

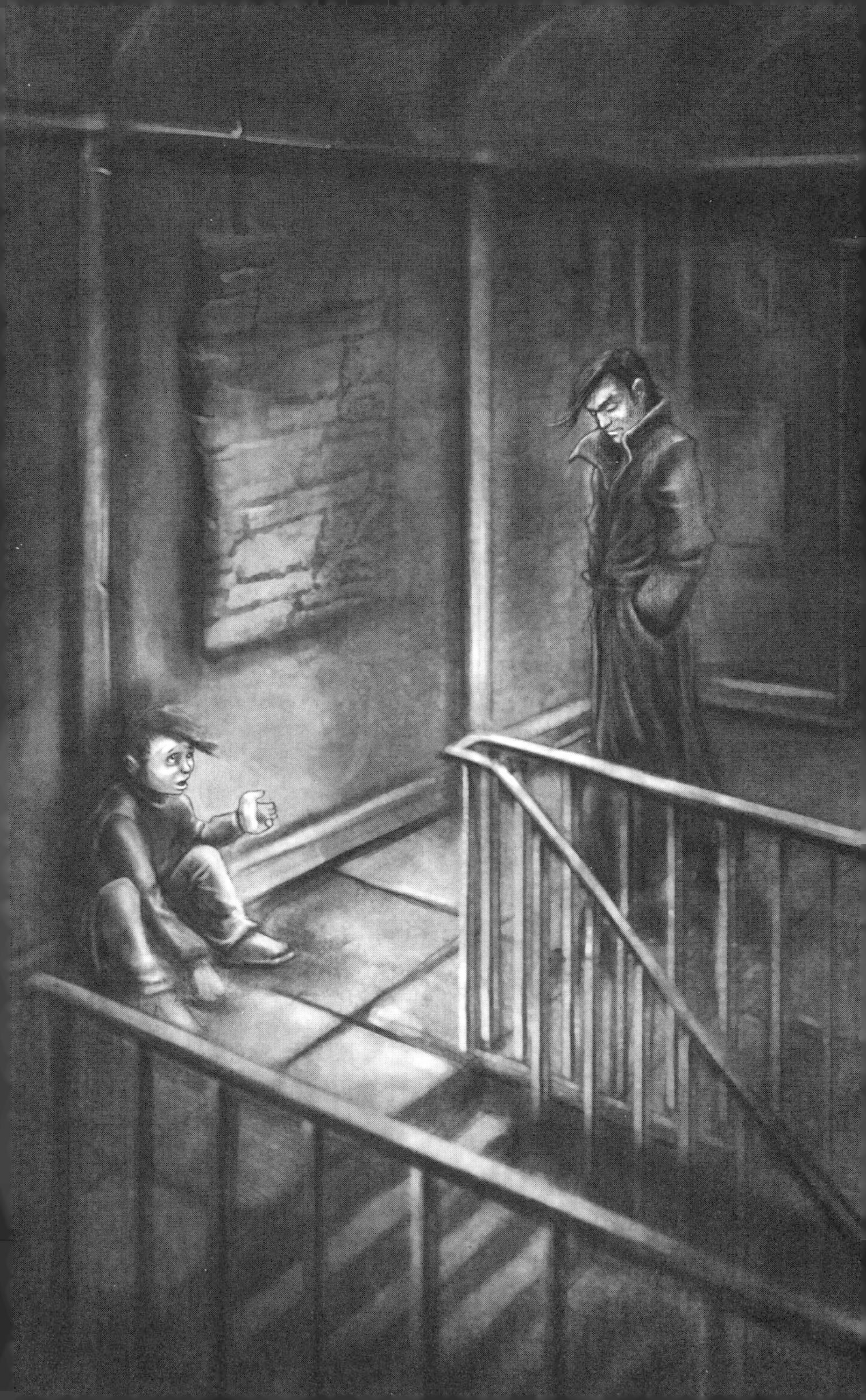

Suddenly, the landing seems darker.

He hears faint sounds of piano music and he has to grip the stair rail.

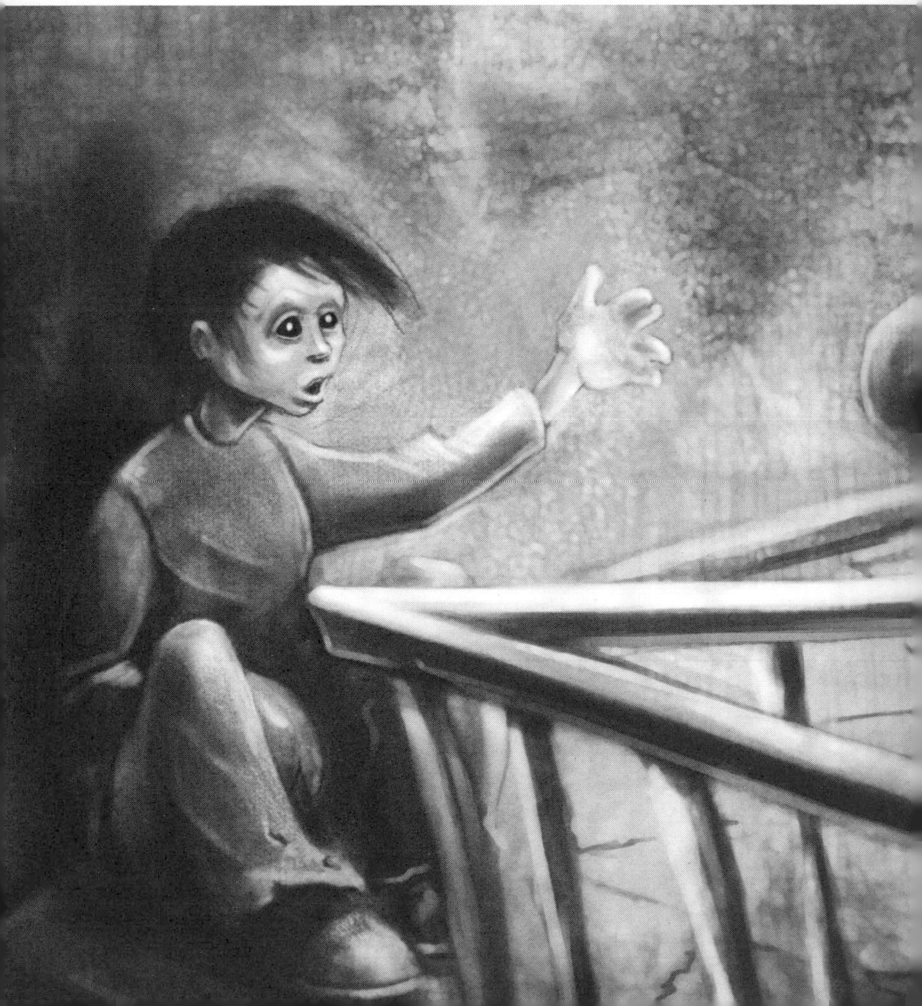

'Only the music lives here,' the little boy says into the gloom.

The Dark Man puts his ear plugs back in.

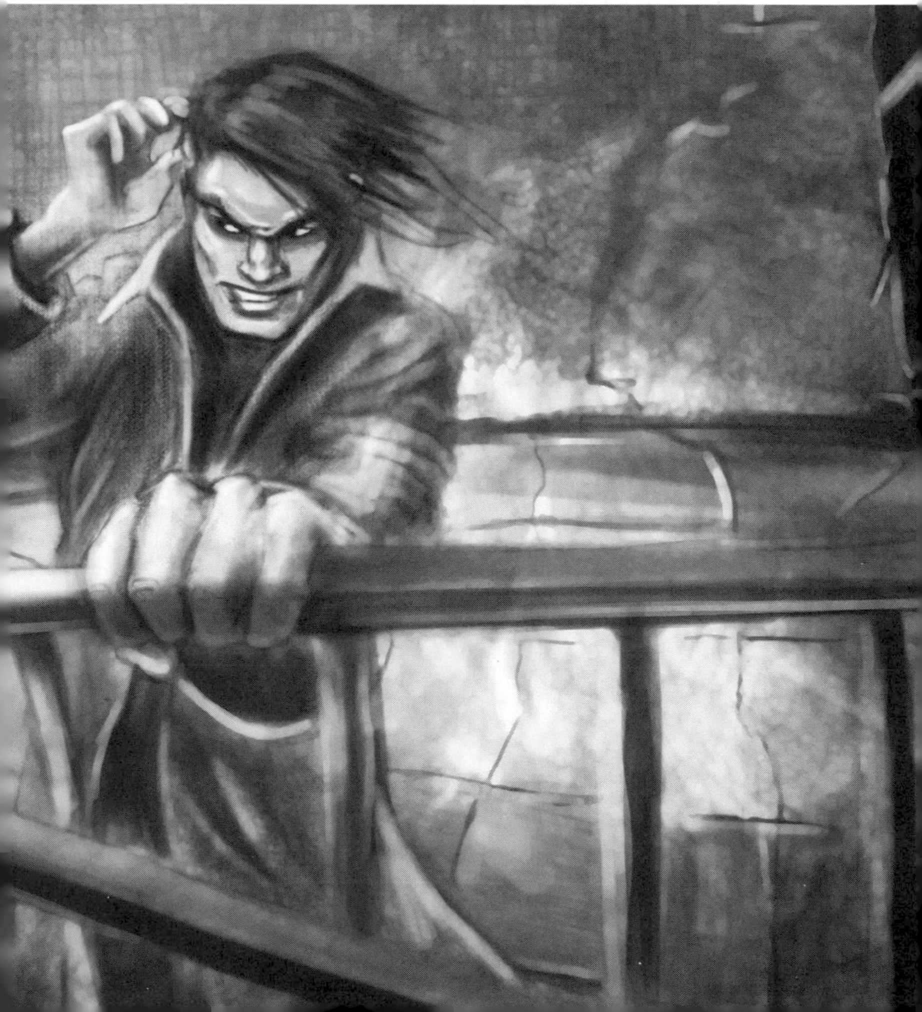

The stairs seem to go up forever, even though, from the outside, the building seemed to be just three floors high.

Some evil force is working in this place.

The Dark Man continues to climb the stairs.

He takes a crystal from his pocket.

The crystal lights the way through the increasing gloom.

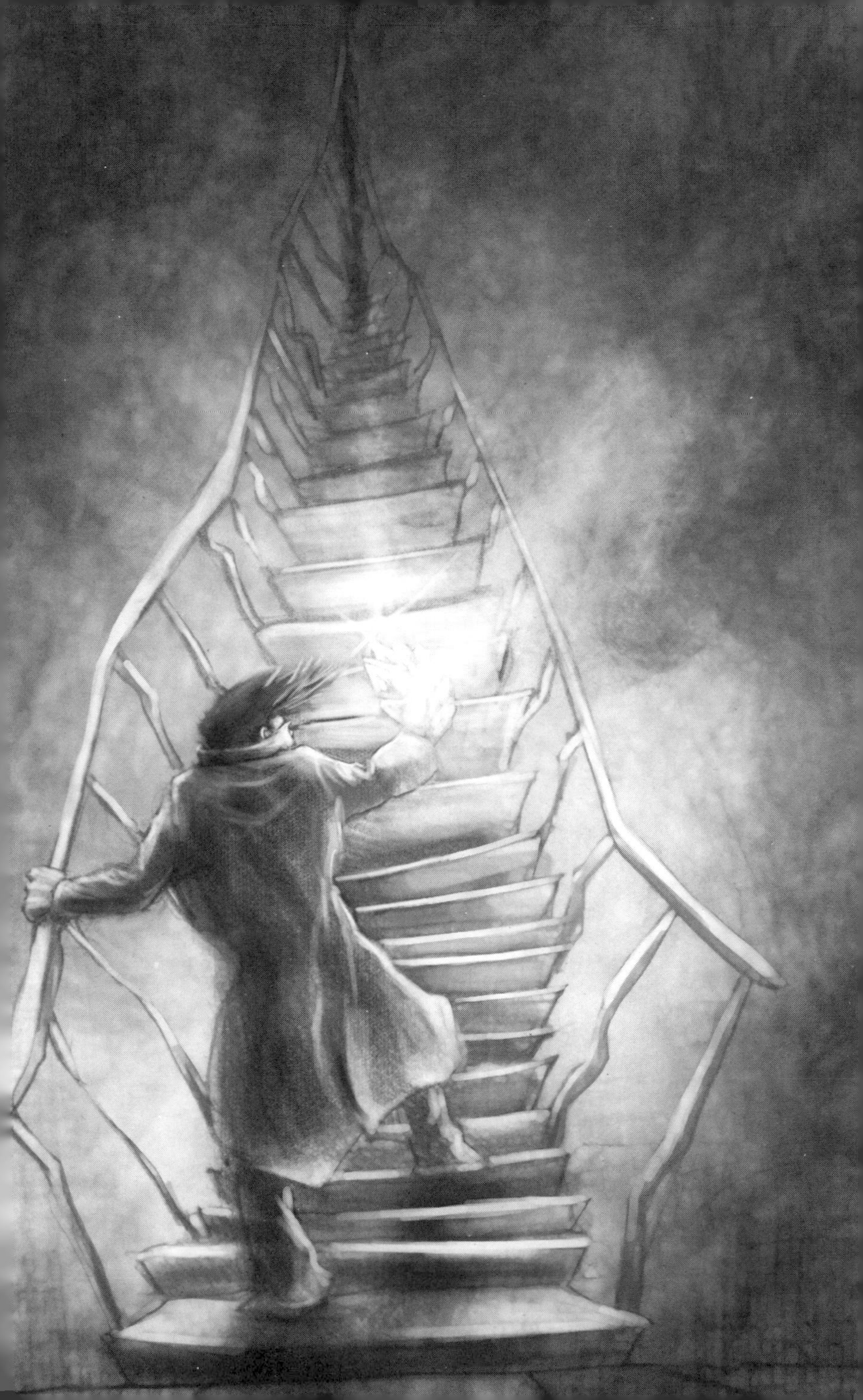

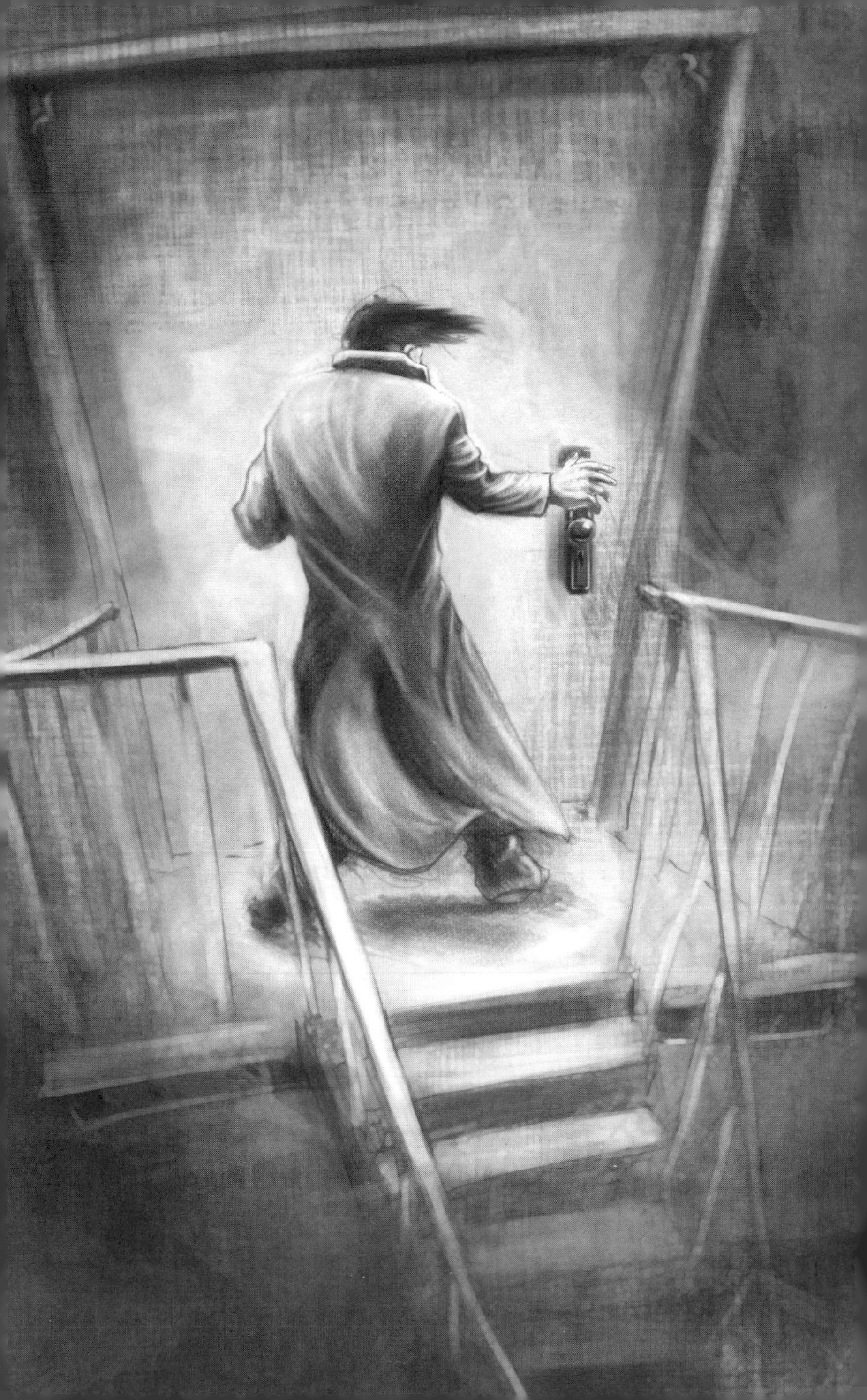

Finally he comes to a landing where the stairs end.

There is just a single doorway.

The music must be coming from there.

He can hear it, even through the ear plugs.

The Dark Man throws the door open.

Inside, the room is in total darkness.

The music compels him to enter, and he thrusts the crystal before him.

But even the crystal can only cast a gloomy light, and the music is stronger than ever.

At the far side of the room is a black, grand piano.

The Dark Man is being pulled towards it.

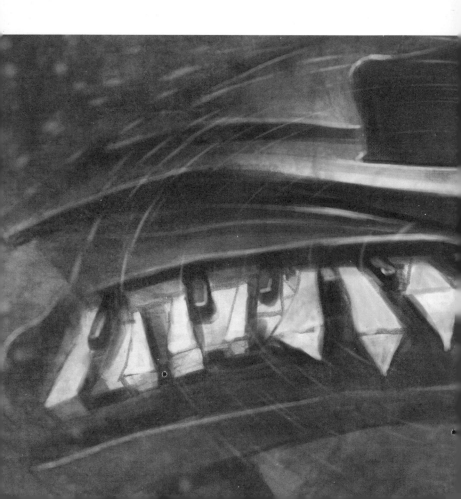

No one is seated at the keyboard, but the keys are working at an impossible speed.

The Dark Man has to fight not to sit at that keyboard.

He feels his fingers drawn towards those hideous keys.

He knows that only light can save him now.

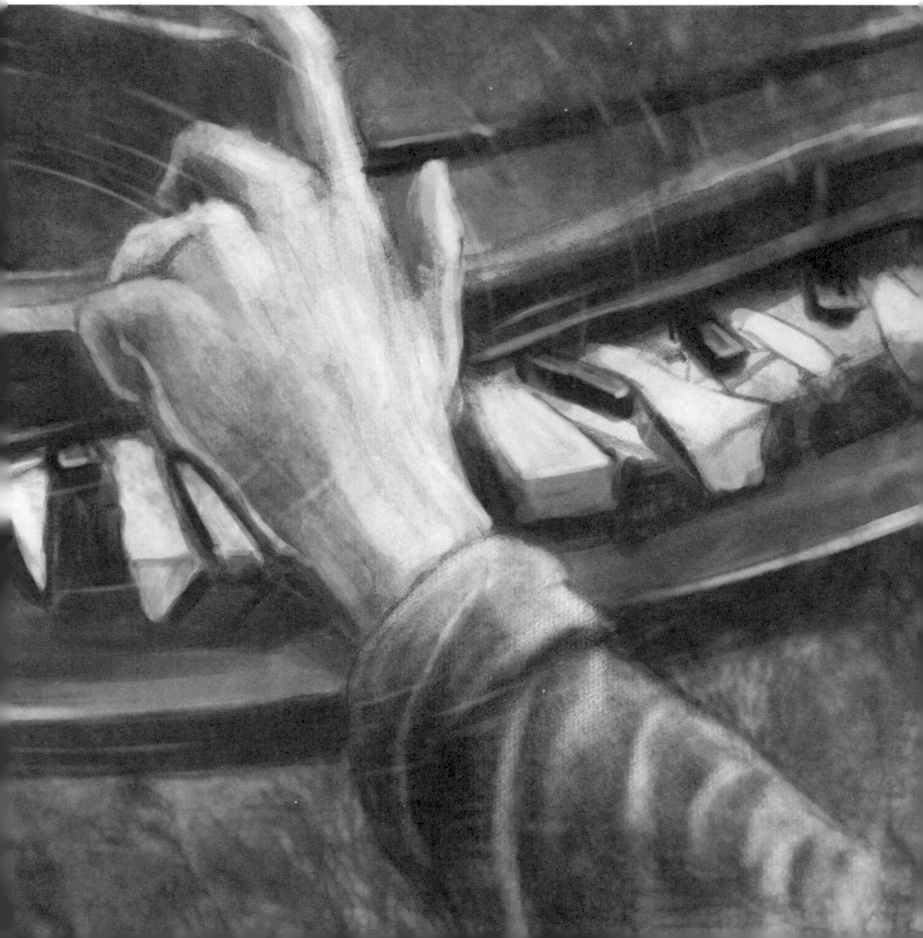

With a mighty effort, he lifts the piano lid.

The music is deafening.

The crystal throbs in his hand and he manages to throw it inside the piano case.

All of a sudden, there is a blinding flash of light and a sound like piano keys wailing.

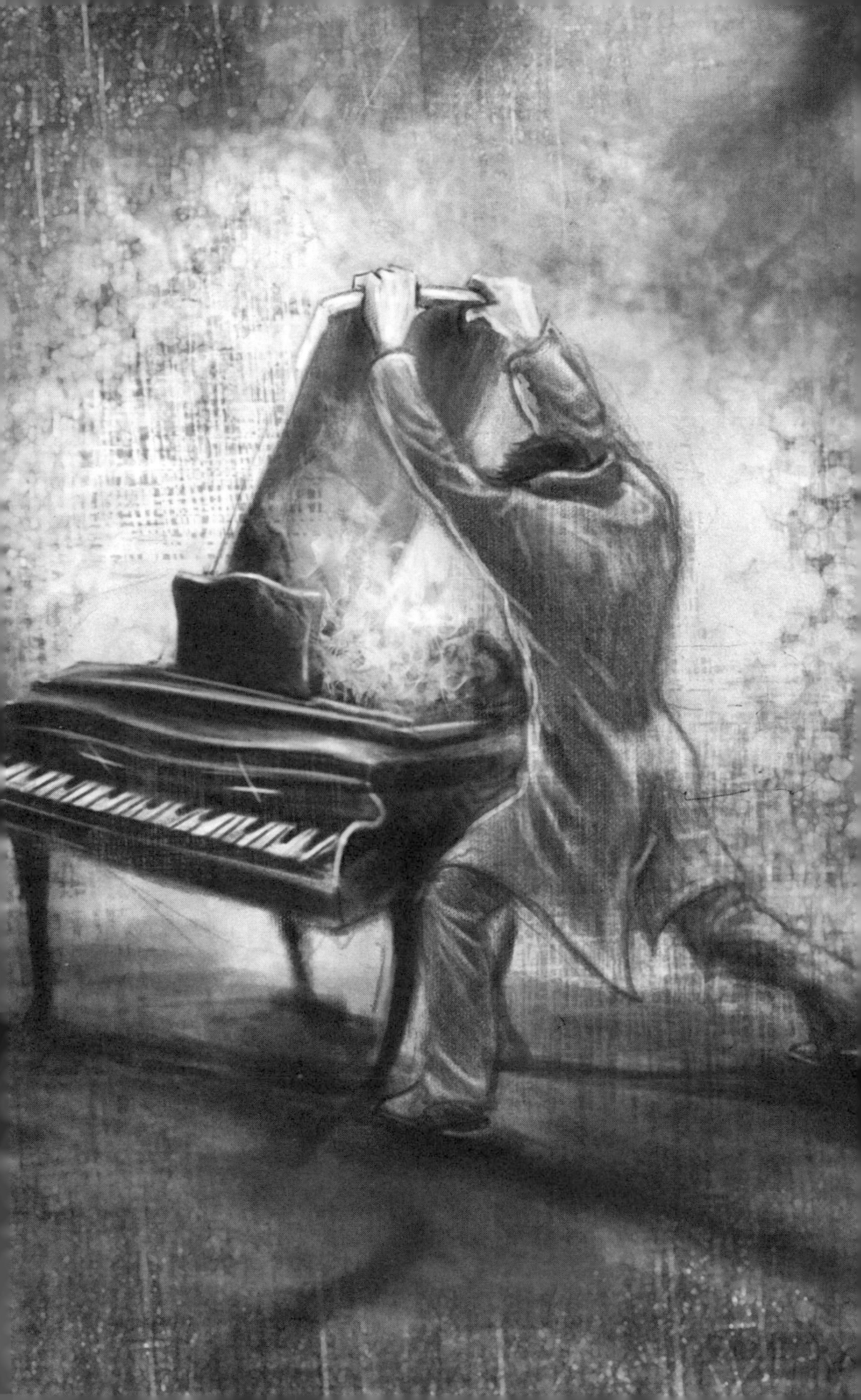

Chapter Four:
The Piano Plays No More

It seems like an age has passed before the Dark Man opens his eyes.

He is sitting in a doorway, opposite the building.

He can no longer hear the music.

The terrible piano plays no more.

As he picks himself up, he wonders how many children the piano had claimed. It saddens his heart.

He makes his way to the building where
Angela lives.

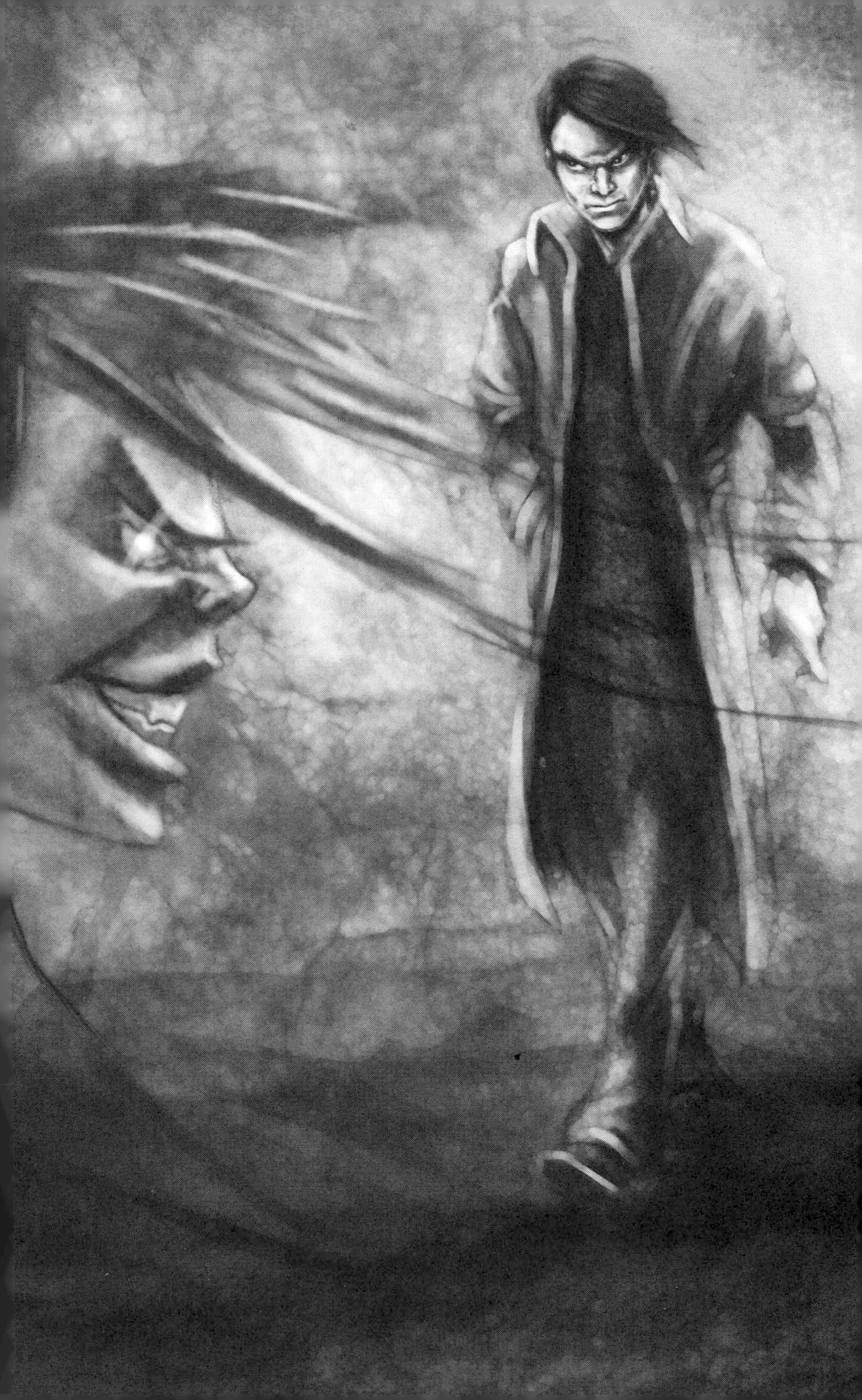

When he gets to her flat, the door is open and Angela is gone.

He will have to find her.

He knows that while Angela roams free, the children of the city will still not be safe.

The author

Peter Lancett is a writer, editor and film maker. He has written many books, and has just made a feature film, *The Xlitherman*.

Peter now lives in New Zealand and California.